Illustrated by Jerrod Maruyama

Customer Service: 1-877-277-9441 or customerservice@pikidsmedia.com

Published by PI Kids, an imprint of Phoenix International Publications, Inc.

8501 West Higgins Road   59 Gloucester Place
Chicago, Illinois 60631   London W1U 8JJ

PI Kids is a trademark of Phoenix International Publications, Inc., and is registered
in the United States.

www.pikidsmedia.com

ISBN: 978-1-5037-5705-9

Disney
My First Stories

HOORAY FOR NATURE!

An imprint of Phoenix International Publications, Inc.

Chicago • London • New York • Hamburg • Mexico City • Sydney

Thumper loves nature! He loves it so much that it makes him thump!

"There's so much to do and see in the forest," he says. "There are flowers to smell, trees to climb, bushes to hide in, and colorful leaves to catch!"

On the winding forest path, Thumper sees Flower the skunk. "Ha-ha," says Thumper, "hee-hee! Who loves nature as much as me?"

"I do!" says the little skunk. "I love sticks and rocks and green grass!"

In the meadow, hidden in the flowers, Thumper plays peek-a-boo with Bambi! "Ha-ha," says Thumper, "hee-hee! Who loves nature as much as me?"

"This butterfly and I do!" says Bambi. "We love the cool forest breeze, fragrant flowers, and buzzing bees!"

Under a rainbow on the grassy field, Thumper greets another bunny. "Ha-ha," says Thumper, "hee-hee! Who loves nature as much as me?"

"I do!" says the little bunny.
"I love sunny days with clear blue
skies and white puffy clouds!"

When it starts to rain in the forest clearing, Thumper sees Friend Owl. "Ha-ha," says Thumper, "hee-hee! Who loves nature as much as me?"

"I do, hoo-hoo!" says Friend Owl. "I love playing in the cool rain and seeing the snails!"

At the pond, Thumper meets the Duck Family. "Ha-ha," says Thumper, "hee-hee! Who loves nature as much as me?"

One little duckling laughs and quacks. "I do!" she says. "I love the pond and all the creatures that live here!"

On the forest path, Thumper sees the Quail Family. "Ha-ha," says Thumper, "hee-hee! Who loves nature as much as me?"

"I do!" says a baby quail. "Come with us, and I'll show you why!"

At the cool, clear river, everyone gathers on the soft, grassy banks.

"Who loves nature as much as we?" the forest friends say. "I do!" shouts Thumper. "Hooray for nature!"